PRAISE FOR DAEDALUS SQUAD

Robert G. Williscroft's *Daedalus Squad* brilliantly advances the missions that readers encountered in the first two stories of the *Daedalus Files*. This time, a six-man squad in improved wingsuits launches into Low Earth Orbit and travels around the globe before landing. Its purpose is to do it eventually under combat conditions. As you might expect, something is bound to go wrong with this training mission, and it does, leading to a tense conclusion.

The near-future scientific and technological detail here is thoroughly convincing. The space hardware involved, especially the improved *Gryphon-10 Mk 4* wingsuit might actually come off the assembly line in a few years, awaiting its first occupant. As in the author's previous stories, maps show the global paths of the men and make it easy to follow their progress in space. At times, you even feel you're along for the ride.

— Professor John B. Rosenman,
Norfolk State University Former Chairman
of the Board, Horror Writers Association Author
of *The Inspector of the Cross Series*

More space-going SEAL action from Robert Williscroft. "Tiger" Baily, the wingsuited, space-jumping hero of Williscroft's *Daedalus Files*, has the stakes upped once again as his whole team makes a jump from orbit in *Daedalus Squad*. This time they're leaving nothing to chance and have already simulated every possible bad-news scenario they can think of. Too bad nature can come up with something they didn't think of. Another fun ride, if your idea of fun includes death-defying action.

— Alastair Mayer
Author of *The T-Space Series*

Daedalus Squad is the latest in a series of tales by Robert G. Williscroft, centered around an experimental Navy SEAL team, the SEALS Winged Insertion Command (SWIC), exploiting a futuristic space launch system to reach Low Earth Orbit—without a rocket.

That technology was well explained in Williscroft's previous novel, *Slingshot*. The *SWIC Daedalus Files* concern the development of special combat operations with easy access to space.

As with most experimental research, in Williscroft's stories, there are challenges—and mishaps galore. In this storyline, with humans hurtling around the Earth at orbital velocities, there is precious little room for error. Controlled re-entry of a human body is even riskier. All of that riskiness translates into an exciting read.

Aside from the thrills inherent in such feats of heroism, this story is educational. If you've wondered how orbiting spacecraft maneuver to change orbits, or rendezvous with other orbiting bodies (in this story, literally human bodies), *Daedalus Squad* will reveal enough of the lingo to help you search online and find out how it's done.

That education alone adds an unexpected dimension to this treasure of a story. You will definitely want to read this one and the next offering in the *SWIC Daedalus Files*.

— Dr. John R. Clarke
Author of *The Jason Parker Series*

This short story by author Robert Williscroft continues the adventures of Lt.Cdr. Derek "Tiger" Baily. Sporting the newest version of the wingsuit (the Gryphon 10 Mk 4), Tiger plans to link up with the other members of his squad in Low Earth Orbit and then descend in formation to a landing at the Amargosa Valley. When the plan goes awry, Tiger must think quickly and use his considerable flying skills to avoid certain death.

The Daedalus adventures, each a short story, follow *Slingshot*, delivering exciting and thought-provoking sci-fi entertainment through the voice of Tiger. Each adventure stands alone, but I'd recommend reading them in order to appreciate how the characters develop.

— Dr. Dave Edlund
***USA Today* Bestselling Author**
The Peter Savage Thrillers

DAEDALUS SQUAD

SWIC Squad Drop from Low Earth Orbit

DAEDALUS SQUAD

SWIC Squad Drop from Low Earth Orbit

Robert G. Williscroft

Guntersville

Daedalus Squad:
SWIC Squad Drop from Low Earth Orbit

Fresh Ink Group
An Imprint of:
The Fresh Ink Group, LLC
1021 Blount Avenue, #931
Guntersville, AL 35976
Email: info@FreshInkGroup.com
FreshInkGroup.com

Edition 1.0 2019

Images by Robert G. Williscroft
Book design by Amit Dey / FIG
Artwork by Anik / FIG
Cover design by Stephen Geez / FIG
Associate publisher Lauren A. Smith / FIG

Keywords: Amelia Earhart Skyport, Australia, Baker Island, Coronado, Fred Noonan Skyport, Free Fall, Gryphon, Hawaii, Howland Island, Hypergolic, Jarvis Island, Keith Lofstrom, Launch Loop, Lagos, Madagascar, Orbit, San Diego, SEALS, Spacesuit, SWIC, Wingsuit

Cataloging-in-Publication Recommendations:
FIC028020 FICTION / Science Fiction / Hard Science Fiction
FIC002000 FICTION / Action & Adventure
FIC028010 FICTION / Science Fiction / Action & Adventure

Library of Congress Control Number: 2019914485

ISBN-13: 978-1-947867-62-8 Papercover
ISBN-13: 978-1-947867-63-5 Hardcover
ISBN-13: 978-1-947867-64-2 Ebooks

DEDICATION

This story is dedicated to the U.S. Navy SEALS who may already be working on a concept like the Gryphon.

TABLE OF CONTENTS

Dedication ix

Acknowledgments xiii

Foreword xv

Cast of Characters xvii

Daedalus Squad 1

- 8,000 Meters Above Death Valley 1
- Coronado—San Diego—Several Days Earlier 1
- Coronado—Gryphon-10 Mk 4 2
- Coronado—Max 3
- Coronado—Squad Drop Prep 4
- Howland & Baker Islands—Prelaunch 4
- Amelia Earhart Skyport—Prelaunch 6
- Amelia Earhart Skyport—Launch 9
- Slingshot Rail 9
- LEO 10
- LEO—Squad Drop 13
- Death Valley—Bird Strike 17
- Death Valley—Snag 18
- Daedalus Squad—Finale 21

Please Post a Review for Daedalus Squad 23
Excerpt from the first chapter of *Slingshot*....24
Words of Praise for Slingshot 33
About Robert G. Williscroft 35
Other books by Robert G. Williscroft 37
Connect with Robert G. Williscroft 39
Daedalus Squad Glossary 40

ACKNOWLEDGEMENTS

Several people contributed to the creation of this series.

Most significantly, my wonderful wife, Jill, whom I first met when I returned from a year at the South Pole conducting atmospheric research, and who finally consented to marry me nearly thirty years later, pored over this story with her discerning engineer's eye. She kept my timeline honest and made sure that regular readers could understand fully the arcane details of the Launch Loop and the Gryphon.

Hard science fiction authors Alastair Mayer, John Clark, and Prof John Rosenman, and USA Today *bestselling author Dave Edlund reviewed the manuscript and offered their editorial insights.*

Lauren Smith from Fresh Ink Group applied her professional associate publisher's eye to improve the story.

It goes without saying that any remaining omissions, errors, and mistakes fall directly on my shoulders.

Robert G. Williscroft, PhD
Centennial, Colorado
October 2019

FOREWORD

Slingshot is my novel about constructing the world's first Space Launch Loop. The book was launched August, 2015, at the International Space Elevator Conference in Seattle, and resides on the desk of every Space Elevator scientist in the world. Space Launch Loops appear in the subsequent books in *The Starchild Trilogy*, and anyone familiar with my *Trilogy* knows all about these commercial space launch systems.

When I discovered the *Gryphon* rigid wingsuit, the *Daedalus* stories pushed themselves into my consciousness. The first story is a consequence of Slingshot's skyports effectively being 80 km tall wingsuit *base-jumping* towers. The second story, *Daedalus LEO*, follows naturally from the first—a drop from Low Earth Orbit (LEO). This story is a consequence of the proof-of-concept LEO drop. In this story, an entire SWIC squad drops from LEO together, in preparation for the final tale, an actual combat drop.

SEAL derring-do is real, the science and technology are real, the *Gryphon* rigid wingsuit is real, and I suspect that something like SWIC will become part of the U.S. Navy SEALS in the relatively near future.

Robert G. Williscroft
Centennial, Colorado
October 2019

CAST OF CHARACTERS

SEALS Winged Insertion Command (SWIC)

Navy Capt. Brad Nelson—Commanding Officer SWIC.

Lt.Cdr. Tom Spitzer—Executive Officer SWIC.

Mother—Controlling computer in each *Gryphon-10*

Max—Full-size *Gryphon-10* simulator

SEALS Winged Insertion Command Three (SWIC-3)

Lt.Cdr. Derek "Tiger" Baily—Narrator, Commanding Officer SWIC-3.

Lt. Jim Fox—Executive Officer SWIC-3.

Master Chief Jerry Boldt—Master Chief SWIC-3.

Senior Chief Bob Baxter—Master Chief Boldt's second.

1st Squad—SWIC-3

Lt. Roger "Rog" Brook—Squad Leader

Chief Douglas Slade

Petty Officer 1st Class Francisco "Jerico" Rodriguez

Petty Officer 1st Class Ronald "Cappy" Caplan

Petty Officer 2nd Class Peter "Pete" Farwall

Not participating in the drop

Petty Officer 2nd Class Benjamin "Benny" Williams

Petty Officer 2nd Class Christopher "Piggy" Pigwell

Petty Officer 3rd Class Clyde "Cowboy" Horseman

Launch Loop International (LLI)

Sam Davidson—Slingshot Director.

Apryl Searson—Chief Diver EMT.

C-130 Hercules

Lt.Col. Randal Dorsey—C-130 Hercules pilot

DAEDALUS SQUAD

8,000 METERS ABOVE DEATH VALLEY

"What the fuck was that?" someone yelled. It sounded like Jerico Rodriguez—a bit of Hispanic twang. Then I heard a loud crunch as my heads-up display went crazy.

"Shit!" I yelped as my hardshell wingsuit commenced rolling hard to the right. Mother automatically torqued my wings to compensate but without much success. I activated my hypergolic rocket, but nothing happened.

I cleared the alarms in my heads-up display and moved them to the right corner. I could see my squad in formation behind me as I lost altitude on a rolling plunge from 8,000 meters. Chief Douglas Slade's blip moved above my position.

"You got a hole the size of Cappy's head in your right wing," he said, referring to Petty Officer First Class Ronald Caplan. "You ain't got no UDMH left."

"Tell me about it," I muttered.

"I got a problem here, Control," I said, trying to keep my voice steady. I briefly described my situation. "I need some immediate help to get out of this."

CORONADO—SAN DIEGO—SEVERAL DAYS EARLIER

Derek "Tiger" Baily again. I suspect you remember my base jump from Fred Noonan Skyport and my LEO drop or you wouldn't be reading this. Have you seen *Gryphon-7* and *Gryphon-10* hanging in the Smithsonian Atrium? They're a bit worse for wear but pretty cool to look at.

I'm still with the Teams—the U.S. Navy SEALS, and continue to command SEALS Winged Insertion Command Three, SWIC-3 for short. The way things are in the military right now, I'm probably stuck with my present rank, Lieutenant-Commander.

We were about to do a proof-of-concept LEO drop with an abbreviated 6-man squad using *Gryphon-10 Mk 4s*. I took the lead on this one, pushing my 1st Squad Leader, Lt. Roger Brook, down into the ranks displacing Petty Officer Clyde Horseman, much to Cowboy's displeasure. Cowboy, as everybody called him, along with Petty Officers Benjamin Williams and Christopher Pigwell—Benny and Piggy to the squad, were on standby in case something went wrong.

CORONADO—GRYPHON-10, MK 4

Gryphon-10 Mk 4 looked exactly like the wingsuit I used for the first LEO drop. It differed in subtle ways, however, because of improvements we developed as I and each of my guys made several LEO drops gaining experience and proficiency along the way.

Beyond that, since we intended to use the *Gryphon* in combat, we incorporated the latest model of a very efficient, hand-held, pulsed energy weapon into a node in the leading edge of either the left or right wing. Its power source is a lightweight BatCap, a unique marriage of a 3-D battery and a thin, large-surface-area flexible capacitor that the SWIC member wears on his back. The capacitor supports twenty rapid-release lethal laser bursts and recharges in less than a minute from the 3-D battery, or it can continuously support a lethal laser burst every five seconds. The 3-D battery needs recharging every five thousand bursts. Before opening the carapace after landing, the SWIC member retrieves the weapon from its node and holsters it just like a sidearm.

Launch pallet improvements ensured that nobody had to go through what happened to me on my first LEO drop. Each pallet carried four tanks. Two were HP oxygen used by the flyer until *Gryphon* separation, attached to the wingsuit with breakaway connectors. The other two carried hypergolic fuel, UDMH and nitrogen tetroxide, for the small hypergolic maneuvering jets that would allow us to get into formation and maintain our pattern until we dropped. Each SWIC-3 team member had completed five LEO drops. Every one of us reached a level of confidence and proficiency as we dealt with problems and solved them on the fly, so to speak. We were as ready as possible for the next step, making a coordinated drop from LEO and landing together at a designated spot on the planet in preparation for doing it for real under combat conditions.

That is, of course, if things went according to plan.

What we were attempting, at least in principle, was straightforward. The six of us would launch in sequence from Amelia Earhart Skyport. Mother would coordinate our detaching from the rail into Hohmann Transfer Orbits (HTO) so that we would find ourselves in a tight group when we reached LEO. From there, at the proper time, we would drop together, again coordinated by Mother, finally landing at our destination, ready to discard our wingsuits to carry out our assigned ground mission or, for that matter, to carry them with us on our backs.

CORONADO—MAX

Max, our full-scale simulator, played a significant role in our preparation. We didn't have the budget for six Max simulators, so we set Max up to simulate a drop of six *Gryphon-10s* with one person at a time in the driver's seat. Each of us ran the Max squad-simulation dozens of times. I did the first run and actually landed the entire squad without a problem. I guess Max was being easy on me because I crashed and burned big-time on my second run. With practice, we all became so proficient that in the end, Max was not able to crash any of us. Remember, however, that Max was only as good as his programming. We entered virtually every kind of possible contingency we could think of, and Max threw every one of them at each of us, singly and in various combinations. Too bad we were not a bit more imaginative thinking up possible things that could go wrong.

Just like on my first LEO drop, however, everything we did up to this point was theoretical, *everything*. As before we not only gave Max every scrap of reentry information we could find, but Max also had everything we had generated with our many LEO drops since then. Max already had everything we knew about upper atmosphere weather and every bit of physics that could possibly bear on the problem. Mother knew everything Max knew and was connected to worldwide live feeds. In our real drop, Mother would know everything possible about the path ahead, and everything Max had done in similar situations during simulation runs. Mother would have every possible edge to give us the desired outcome. Yet...until we actually made the first squad drop, all we had were numbers that we hoped made sense.

CORONADO—SQUAD DROP PREP

We had reached a level of experience and proficiency so that we no longer set up a backup unit for each of our drops. As always, each man was ultimately responsible for his own *Gryphon*. Before we loaded the six units on the waiting Navy jet transport, Master Chief Boldt and I inspected each unit, carefully and completely. Then each team member inspected his own unit again. This was the big one—failure was not an option.

Capt. Nelson maintained his high-level discussions with his Team boss. On this morning, Capt. Nelson informed me that the White House would be watching on an encrypted holobroadcast. Apparently, the Commander-in-Chief was a frustrated wingsuit flyer wannabe.

HOWLAND & BAKER ISLANDS—PRELAUNCH

I departed Coronado for North Island Airfield with Senior Chief Baxter and the entire First Squad plus three guys from Second Squad. I wanted one man assisting each flyer with the Senior Chief in charge. We were pretty busy, and I don't remember saying anything witty as I had done on our departure for the first LEO drop. I do recall thinking that this would be a piece of cake. Good thing I didn't say that out loud, as it turned out.

Trips to Howland Island on the Navy supersonic transport were becoming pretty routine. This one was no different. We jetted down the runway, lifted through sparse clouds into a brilliant blue stratosphere, leaving a layer of puffy cirrocumulus clouds far below us. We turned toward Hawaii as we accelerated to nearly Mach 2.

I slept right through our refueling stop in Hawaii, waking up as we rolled to a stop at Amelia Earhart International Airport under a blistering equatorial sun. As if they were greeting my return, thousands of sooty terns, lesser frigatebirds, and masked boobies filled the sky, kept clear of aircraft by built-in sonic systems.

Apryl Searson met me at the ramp, her pixie blond hair, and thin, short dress fluttering in the tropical breeze. She took my arm and walked me to the Launch Loop International (LLI) Howland headquarters building where she had already prepared an appropriate place to greet me properly. By now, these trysts were legendary in SWIC, but none of the guys begrudged me my good fortune. Actually, the pickings were sufficiently slim and the schedule so tight, that they really had no chance.

At the end of the tarmac, LLI's two Chinooks waited with cargo bays open, twin rotors seemingly wilting in the hot tropical sun. Senior Chief Baxter and his six guys unloaded the six pallets with help from Lt. Brook and the other flyers and then loaded two into the Chinooks. They all accompanied the first two pallets to Baker. And then returned for two more, and then for the remaining two.

✷

I spent a few minutes with Sam Davidson, the local LLI Director, bringing him up to date on what we were doing. He had been following our activities closely, and probably was as anxious as the rest of us for the success of this next step. Now that the Atlantic Launch Loop was in operation, Slingshot had a bit less pressure on its 24/7 schedule of throwing people and cargo into space. No matter how you cut it though, Sam was launching 2,000 metric tons of cargo and eighty personnel capsules into space every day.

"Where is all that stuff going, Sam?" I asked as I stood to leave.

"Out there," Sam said with a grin gesturing toward the ceiling and slapped my back, something that was becoming a ritual. "Good luck, Tiger! Like I've told you each time we meet like this, I'm glad it's you, and not me."

✷

This time around, Apryl accompanied me to Baker Island in the last Chinook. Senior Chief Baxter joined us. Even with the pallet, the three of us had plenty of room. The rest of the guys had crowded around the pallet in the other Chinook.

"Nice to see you, Miss Apryl," Baxter said, his eyes twinkling.

"And you, Senior Chief," Apryl said, kissing his cheek as he blushed crimson. Apryl giggled, kissed him again, and snuggled back beside me.

After we landed at Baker, Apryl and I, accompanied by the other five flyers, took the five-minute trip in a personnel capsule up to Amelia Earhart Skyport. Meanwhile, under Senior Chief Baxter's supervision, the articulating boom crane loader hoisted the pallets over the rail where a crew member attached each to a launch dolly. The process had become pretty routine, but the Senior Chief never let his attention wander during the loading.

AMELIA EARHART SKYPORT—PRELAUNCH

At Amelia Earhart Skyport, our capsule tilted to horizontal, sealed against the skyport lock, and the door opened inward. Apryl and I stepped into the reception area, followed by my guys. The capsule closed behind us, and the lock sealed. Apryl took a seat against the outer wall, and I addressed my team.

"You've all done this before, but individually. Anything happens like it did with Cappy or me, you got more to think of than yourself. We're back to being a team, a fighting team—even though this is just a drill." I got a chuckle from the five in front of me. "Know your position in the formation at all times. If a teammate gets into trouble and you can help, do so! But don't risk everyone in the process. Remember, with this exercise we're showing the mucky-mucks that SWIC is a viable insertion tool, perhaps the best we've ever developed."

"Hooyah!" Chief Slade responded, joined by the rest, me included, "Hooyah!"

"Okay, guys, suit up!" Slade ordered, and a minute or so later, the first pallet arrived.

With skytower traffic stopped, all the guys except me hustled through the personnel lock. They removed the fairing and stowed it, and then they prepped the pallet with its *Gryphon* payload, swinging the wingsuit pod cover to vertical on its hinges like a clamshell. Slade examined every part of the pallet and wingsuit. He was quick but efficient, mindful of the queued-up freight pallets and passenger capsules waiting down at Baker Socket. As he finished, he signaled Lt. Roger Brook to do his final system check. Rog, as we called him, had looked over Slade's shoulder through his entire system check, so he was certain that everything was ready, but he still went through the list just to make sure.

Rog stepped up on his *Gryphon*, backed against the carapace cover, and one of the guys secured his legs and torso and lowered him into the wingsuit.

"Time to go," I said to Apryl, who was snuggled against me on the same couch we used before my first LEO drop. The Milky Way, that multi-colored diamond-studded bracelet spanning the sky, was as awesome as ever, taking my breath away as I untangled myself from Apryl.

Apryl kissed me passionately. "Be safe, Tiger…I worry about you."

Of course, we had no idea what lay before me.

✵

I suited up quickly. Our lightweight suits incorporated high-pressure oxygen bottles, electronic carbon-dioxide scrubbers, and TBH jet boots that slipped over the suit feet and calves.

I stepped through the personnel lock onto the dock just as Rog's pallet disappeared around the bend to receive kick thruster and launch dolly.

The second pallet arrived, followed almost immediately by a personnel capsule carrying Baxter and his crew. They disembarked into the Skyport lounge where they suited up and joined us on the dock as Chief Slade's pallet queued up at the end of the dock. We had room for three pallets in queue before we had to launch the first. We generally knew the sequence, but Mother would coordinate the entire operation, based upon the time of the first launch, the times of each subsequent inspection and launch, and when each pallet was released to its specific HTO. The biggest potential variable was how long it took to inspect each pallet, load the flyer, and put him in the queue.

We had practiced the sequence often enough back in Coronado so that we actually worked like an oiled machine. I say *we*, but that's not quite fair. It was the guys under Senior Chief Baxter's watchful eye who pulled it off. Even though I commanded SWIC-3, up there, right then, I was just an observant passenger.

Petty Officer First Class Francisco Rodriguez—Jerico for some unknown reason—conducted his inspection and was snugged into his *Gryphon*. His pallet joined the queue.

Next up, Petty Officer First Class Ronald Caplan. Cappy, as the guys called him, had already experienced one mishap during LEO drops. From his perspective, this drop had to be perfect. His inspection lasted somewhat longer than the others, but that was fine—no one begrudged him the extra time. Baxter looked at me even though it wasn't necessary. Up here, he was in charge. I nodded, and he signaled to launch Rog down the rail, making room for Cappy's pallet.

Petty Officer Second Class Peter Farwall was next, and I followed Pete. Like Cappy, I inspected my pallet and *Gryphon* with extra care. I certainly didn't want any problems this time.

I stepped onto the pallet, backed up against the pod cover, and allowed the crew to strap me in; the process almost felt normal. Then the crew swung down the pod cover and me, sealed the edges all around, pressurized it, and checked for leaks. The gantry moved me to the end of the queue while Pete received his kick thruster and launch dolly.

AMELIA EARHART SKYPORT—LAUNCH

"Control, this is Tiger—comm check," I said as I felt the kick thruster attach.

"Loud and clear, Tiger," Master Chief Boldt responded. "Just like old times." As always, his calm voice was reassuring.

"Mother, state your status," Boldt ordered.

"Rog, Slade, Jerico, Cappy, and Pete are down the rail. Rog and Slade are in HTO. Standing by to launch Tiger. You," she added as an afterthought. Mother's voice was business-like but still had a soothing, contralto tone.

"Ready when you are," Boldt said.

I felt the gantry lower my pallet to the rail. I was snug as a caterpillar inside my *Gryphon* cocoon. It felt warm and comfortable.

"On my count," Master Chief Boldt said. "Five, four, three, two, one… Launch!"

SLINGSHOT RAIL

As I surged forward, I reminded myself that this was my sixth time down the rail. Staying relaxed, even in tough circumstances, has always come easy to me. By now, this was a piece of cake, except my right buttock started to itch. My arms were free to move inside the *Gryphon* wings, but try as hard as I might, I couldn't reach the itch. I finally moved my rump up against the carapace cover and wiggled. Getting that itch was blessed relief.

Exactly four minutes and ten seconds after launch, Mother rotated my pallet 30° to the left. Thirty-three seconds later and 1,328 klicks down the rail from Amelia Earhart Skyport, Mother released my pallet from the rail and initiated a two-minute-fifteen-second kick thruster burn. At the end of that time, the magnetic iris sliced through the kick thruster's solid fuel stack, cutting off the burn. The pallet with me in my *Gryphon* headed on a path away from the Earth at almost 8 km/s that passed 290 klicks to the north and 19 klicks above Fred Noonan Skyport, and that would intersect the 160 klick orbit on the other side of the Earth at the same point and same time the other five converged. When the acceleration ceased, I relaxed into freefall, fondly remembering Apryl's ministrations in the LLI Admin Building on Howland Island and her Skyport-kiss just before I suited up.

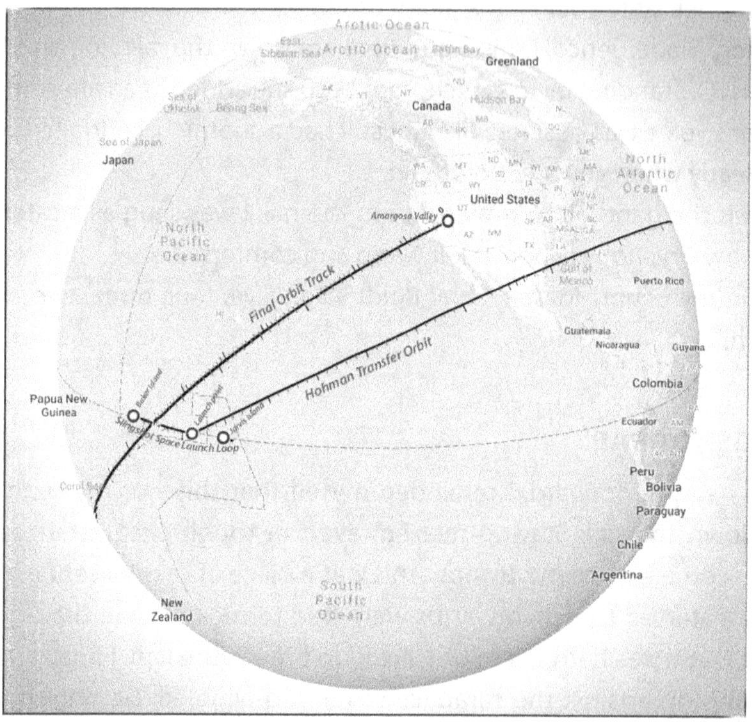

Slingshot Space Launch Loop with the Hohmann Transfer Orbit and the last leg of the final orbit track from Australia to the final landing at Amargosa Valley.

LEO

By now this was old hat. I was in an elliptical HTO with perigee at 80 klicks and apogee at 160 klicks—just like the other five times. The one big difference, however, is that when I reached apogee on the opposite side of the Earth, the rest of my team would be clustered together waiting for me—at least that was the plan.

Time to determine the status and get things organized. "Control, this is Tiger…status of rendezvous," I requested.

"Rog and Slade are at the assembly point," Mother answered. "Jerico is approaching, arrival in twelve minutes. Cappy is eighteen minutes out, Pete is twenty-five minutes out, and you are thirty-nine minutes out."

Do you have any idea how long thirty-nine minutes can be? I remembered sitting on a small stool in my mother's kitchen as a four-year-old watching the wall clock. My mother had said that we would leave when the big hand reached twelve. Those forty minutes took forever, but these thirty-nine minutes took even longer. And to complicate the matter, that itch came back. At least, this time, I knew how to fix it. The upside of this wait was that I had time to admire the Earth below.

On each set of LEO drops, we had set ourselves on different orbital paths, landing twice in the US, once in Africa, once in Australia, and one water-landing near the Soloman Islands in the South Pacific. This time we were following our original orbit fairly closely, planning on landing together in the Amargosa Valley, 145 klicks northwest of Vegas.

As I climbed higher along my HTO, while I played tag with my itch, I had a grand view of the Earth below, but I no longer felt compelled to give Control a blow-by-blow show-and-tell. Baja was covered with clouds, but I knew it was below because Mother had superimposed a map over my heads-up display. Amazingly, Laguna de Myrán, half-way between the Pacific and Atlantic in central Mexico was filled with water for the first time in years. A swirling tropical storm system off New Orleans made me happy that was not my destination. For a change, the Atlantic was about as empty of cloud cover as it ever gets, giving me a grand view of horizon-to-horizon ocean blue until I ran into the terminator about half-way across. I crossed the African coast just south of Mauritania heading toward Lagos, Nigeria's largest city, already a shining diamond on the nighttime horizon.

As I approached Lagos below me, my heads-up display showed my five companions up ahead and above waiting patiently for my arrival.

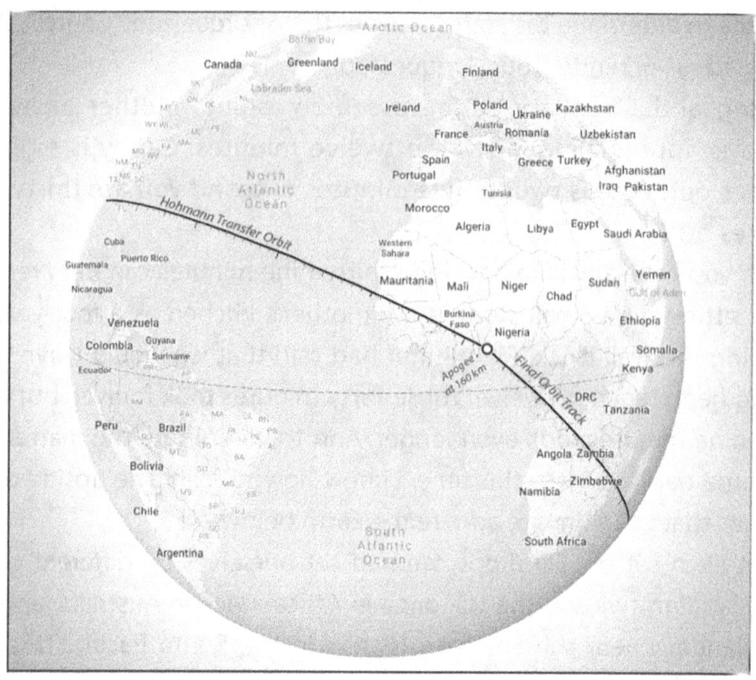

Hohmann Transfer Orbit to the apogee over Lagos. Final circularized orbit track from apogee.

"Squad, this is Tiger. I'm on approach, five minutes out."

"Tiger, this is Rog…we see you in heads-up. You're not yet physically visible. Are your red-green flashers on?"

"They are," I answered, and then I was able to pick out their five sets of flashers against the stars. "I have visible on you," I said.

"I will park you fifty meters below the formation," Mother interrupted. "Stand by for circularizing burn."

Mother ignited the kick thruster for a few seconds—thank goodness nothing went wrong this time. I rubbed my buttock against the carapace cover as I checked my heads-up. The five team members were arrayed above me in a triangular formation with the point missing. That was my slot. Twelve meters separated each pallet horizontally, and three meters vertically. Slade and Jerico filled row two above and behind point, and Cappy, Rog, and Pete made up row three above and behind row two.

Using my maneuvering jets, I brought my pallet to the point position ahead of and three meters below Slade and Jerico. I could have let Mother do this, but I thought it was a great opportunity to show off a bit. We were ready to go.

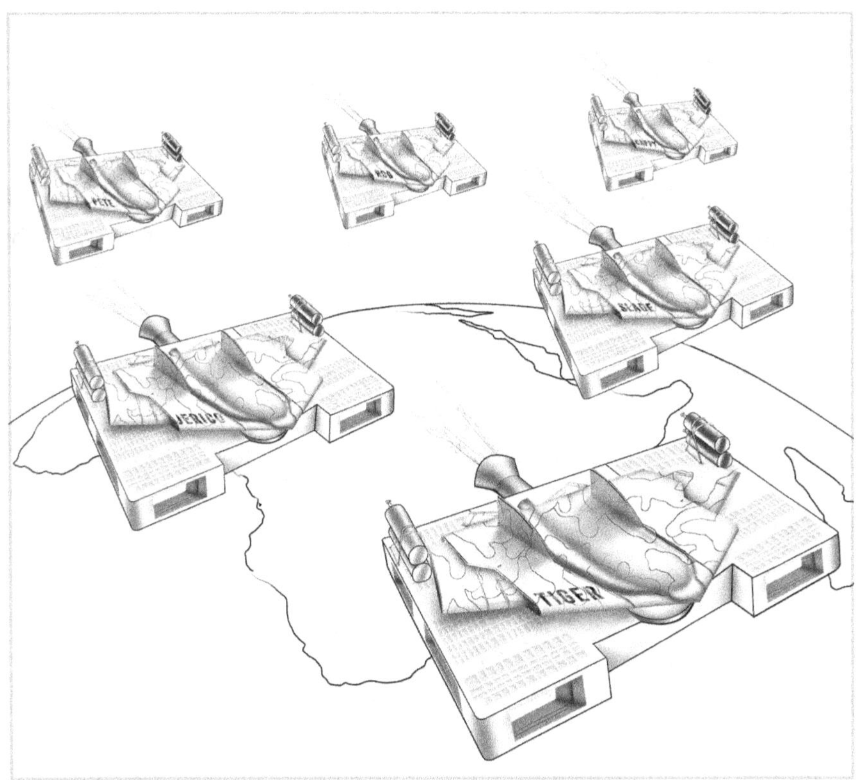

LEO—SQUAD DROP

"Mother, update status," I ordered.

"Fifty-two minutes until squad drop," she answered.

"Control, this is Tiger. I'm going to do the one-eighty now while we're hanging loose."

"Roger that, Tiger. Let Mother handle it."

And she did. Synchronously, Mother rotated all six pallets with their gyros. I watched the eerie dance on my heads-up. If I hadn't known better, I would have taken it for a video game.

"Everybody good?" I asked casually, knowing that my guys were focused—perhaps too much since we were still forty-five minutes to the drop.

"Rog good!"

"Slade okay!"

"Jerico A-OK, Boss!"

"Cappy is fine!"

"Pete too!"

Ten minutes later we met the morning terminator as we passed south of Madagascar, its visible southern tip brown and dry, rising out of the deep blue ocean to the north.

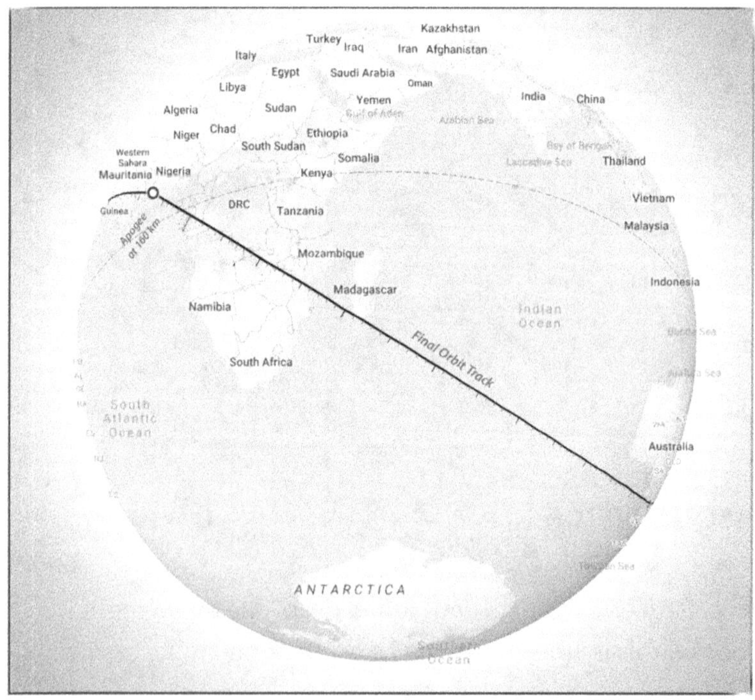

Final orbit track over the Indian Ocean to Australia.

"Let's drop down there and take us a vacation," Jerico said. "Never been there...looks like an interesting place."

"Too late for this orbit," Cappy quipped. "Gotta go around again and commence our drop over western Zimbabwe."

"Might not be welcome there," Pete said. "I hear they don't like people like us..."

"Cut the chatter!" Chief Slade snapped.

Seventeen minutes of empty Indian Ocean later, except for some streaky clouds that looked like they were trying to form a tropical storm, we crossed the Australian coast just south of Adelaide. I played tag with my itch for the entire three minutes we took to cross over New South Wales to the east coast just south of Brisbane. That left us about twenty minutes of South Pacific Islands and open ocean before we commenced our drop.

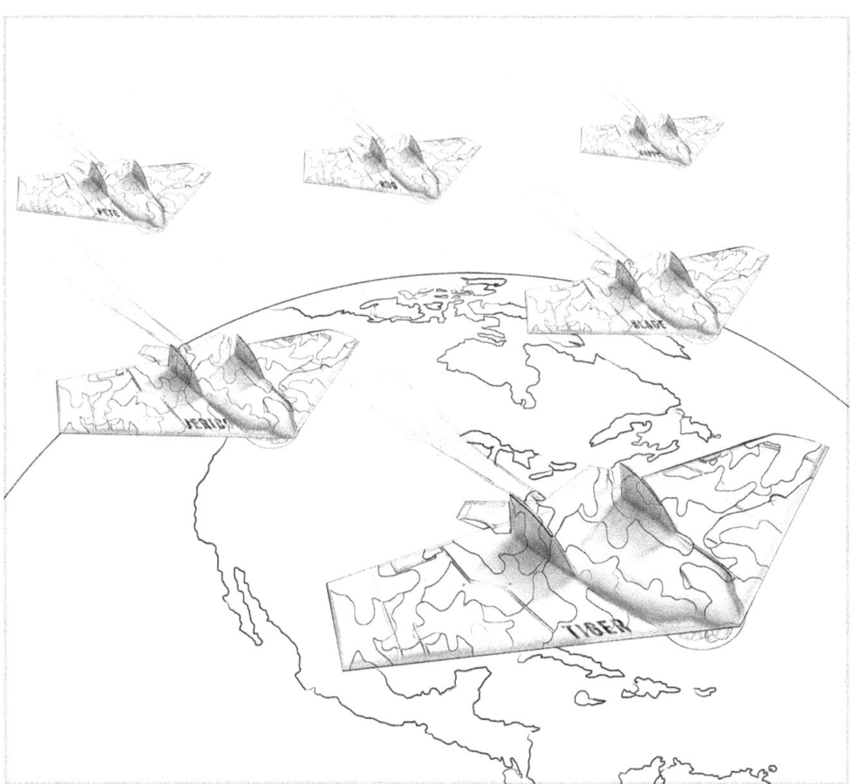

Things seemed to be going pretty well. Snug in my *Gryphon* cacoon, I was feeling more confident with each passing island, each Pacific squall, and each wide open patch of Pacific blue.

✺

By the time we were five minutes out—that's 2,500 klicks—I began to feel a bit of…I wouldn't call it anxiety…more like intense anticipation. I wanted to get the show on the road, itch or no itch.

"Standby," Mother said at the one-minute mark.

Based on her precise calculations, Mother actually commenced the retro-burn about ten seconds earlier than our plan called for, but I was confident. She knew what she was doing. Two minutes or so later—you'll have to examine the log to get the exact number—Mother cut the kick thruster burn and rotated the pallets back, so we were pointed in our direction of travel.

"Good luck and Godspeed!" Master Chief Boldt said as I felt the jolt of pallet separation and on my heads-up watched six expended pallets drop away to burn up in the atmosphere.

"Forward velocity six-eight-hundred meters-per-second," Mother told me. I knew she was also talking to the rest of my squad, and I trusted that she was doing whatever was necessary to keep us in formation. On my heads-up, I saw the individual *Gryphons* increasing their separation until we each were a hundred meters distant from the closest *Gryphon*.

We were accelerating toward the ocean at 9.8 m/sec^2 while heading toward the horizon at 6,800 m/sec. Mother had set a timer when she separated my pallet. Drop timer digits flashed at the right side of my display. At the three-minute mark, the California coast was fifty klicks below, and ten seconds later, we began to grab atmosphere. As things started to heat up, I checked our formation. We still held position. "Report!" I ordered.

"Rog warmin' up!"

"Slade toasty!"

"Jerico friggin' hot, Boss!"

"Cappy ditto!"

"Pete too!"

"Take us up, Mother," I said. Okay thus far. I was feeling pretty good about it.

Mother had already set our nozzles and wing torques to optimize our return to space. I felt weight return and then disappear as Mother cut the burn and announced, "Forward velocity five-zero-eight meters-per-second, net forward transfer nine-three-zero kilometers."

Given what we were doing, that was about as close to being on the button as possible.

Mother reset the timer as our vertical motion slowed to zero, and then together we plunged back into the atmosphere, slowing down to about Mach 14 and eating up another 700 klicks before it got too hot to continue. By the time we dove into our third dip, we were down to Mach 5, and the guys were letting go *Hooyahs* as we whipped back out for the last time.

"Stay focused!" I ordered. I really didn't want something to go wrong this far into the exercise.

The next drop put us at thirty-five klicks above and 150 klicks west of our drop zone at sixty m/sec. It took us a few minutes to work our way down to 8,000 meters above Death Valley. Our destination lay about 50 klicks due east in the Amargosa Valley

We had made it. All that remained was landing and hitching a ride to Vegas. And that's when all hell broke loose!

DEATH VALLEY—BIRD STRIKE

"What the fuck was that?" Jerico yelled, his Hispanic twang quite evident. Then I heard a loud crunch as my heads-up display went crazy.

"Shit!" I yelped as my *Gryphon* commenced rolling hard to the right. Mother automatically torqued my wings to compensate but without much success. I activated my hypergolic rocket, but nothing happened.

I cleared the alarms in my heads-up display and moved them to the right corner. I could see my squad in formation behind me as I lost altitude on a rolling plunge from 8,000 meters. Chief Slade's blip moved above my position.

"You got a hole the size of Cappy's head in your right wing," he said. "You ain't got no UDMH left."

"Tell me about it," I muttered.

"I got a problem here, Control," I said, trying to keep my voice steady. I briefly described my situation. "I will need some immediate help to get out of this."

✺

"I gotcha, Tiger," Jerico said as he maneuvered alongside me, matched my roll, and slipped his left wing under my damaged right. This was something we had never practiced, but Jerico was the best flyer in SWIC, next to me, of course. He stopped my roll and stabilized my wingsuit. I could almost feel stability flowing from his wing to mine.

"Mother, work both units as one," I ordered. And to Jerico, "Think we can make Amargosa Valley?"

"We ain't goin' nowhere but down, Boss," Jerico said to me. "Ain't never been to Death Valley."

As we flew together, I could feel his wing varying pressure against mine as surrounding air currents buffeted our ungainly marriage.

"Rog," I ordered, "take command and complete the mission. Set down in Amargosa Valley as planned. Jerico and I are taking a detour."

DEATH VALLEY SNAG

The *Gryphon-10* has a glide ratio of 14 to 1, meaning that for every meter we dropped, we moved fourteen forward. My *Gryphon* and Jerico's flying together didn't come close to that.

"What's our glide ratio, Mother," I asked.

"Five to one," she answered.

I glanced at my altitude gauge. It read 7,000 meters. That gave us a thirty-five klick range. My stomach dropped, and my itch returned.

"High mountains to the east and really high mountains to the west," I said to Jerico. "We can't make it over the eastern range. We gotta land in Death Valley. It's gonna be a hard landing, but you can pull up at the last moment with your rocket and come in easy. We really got no choice."

Jerico grunted a non-response. He was working pretty hard keeping his wing in contact with mine.

"This is Control," Master Chief Boldt said. "Actually, you do…have a choice, I mean. I got an Air Force C-130 Herc ten minutes out. He's gonna set up so you can fly right into his cargo bay."

"Beats crash landing in Death Valley," I said.

"Hooyah!" Jerico muttered quietly.

✷

Eight minutes later, the lumbering aircraft hove into view, pulled in front of us, and matched our speed and drop rate.

"Tiger, this is Randy Dorsey. Here's what we're gonna do." In just a few seconds, he laid out the plan for us.

"You ready to do this, Jerico?" I asked.

"Hooyah!" he said.

"I'm slowing, Tiger," Dorsey said as he lowered his cargo ramp.

We began to drift toward the open maw of the Herc. It looked pretty small from where we were.

"Slowing more," Dorsey said. We drifted closer—fifty meters out.

"Ten-knot difference between us," Dorsey said.

Twenty-five meters…

"Eight-knot difference…"

Twenty meters…I checked my altitude. Only 2,000 meters. We were below the mountain peaks on either side of us.

"Five-knot difference…"

Five meters out…

"Three-knot difference…"

We were over the ramp, Mother maneuvering us by torquing my left and Jerico's right wings. Suddenly, the big aircraft dropped three meters. One moment we were ready to set down on the ramp, the next, the Herc was falling away below us. We got separated by the turbulence from this lumbering beast, and I did a complete rollover before Jerico synched to my movement and slipped his left wing back under my right.

"Thanks, Jerico, that feels good!"

"Hooyah!" Jerico grunted as he fought to keep us together. Mother dropped us back and down to the Herc's level. Fleeting images of Apryl whipped across my mind as we struggled to hold the *Gryphons* together.

"Let's give it another go, Randy," I said, forcing my voice to remain calm like the cool fighter pilots in holovision broadcasts.

"Roger that, Tiger. Ready to try again. The road is a bit bumpy, so stay alert!"

Once more, we aimed at the cargo opening, Mother keeping us to the right.

"Back off!" Randy ordered as the Herc bounced up about a meter. Apparently, Mother saw it coming because she dropped us back and away from the ramp.

"Okay," Randy said, "bring her in now!"

With some remaining forward motion and the ramp just a meter below us, we reached the forward-right edge of the ramp. My right wing and all of Jerico extended off the ramp's right side. Jerico dropped and pulled away as my lower carapace and both wings hit the ramp. My forward motion caused my right-wing to strike the cargo hatch edge, spinning me clockwise into the hold.

As Jerico dropped his nose, he said, "I can't make it to Amargosa, and I ain't gonna land in no fricken Death Valley." He did a full 360 on his rocket, flew toward the ramp, and slid into the C-130 cargo hold, retracting his wings as he did so.

"Nice flyin'," Dorsey said as he closed the ramp.

DAEDALUS SQUAD—FINALE

Rog and the rest of the squad landed without incident in Amargosa Valley a stone's throw from some kind of a mechanized dairy farm. We met the next day in Vegas, where we celebrated as only sailors can.

Oh yeah, about what happened over Death Valley...You may not believe this, but we ran into a flock of migrating geese, at 8,000 meters no less. Who tracks migrating geese? Especially at 8,000 meters? They've been seen before at this altitude, but it's rare. Their presence over Death Valley at our arrival was a complete fluke. They were doing 10 kph; we were doing about 200. They lost one of theirs, and we almost lost me. I guess we both were lucky.

This time we actually managed to keep our exploit secret. The Commander-in-Chief was delighted with the proof-of-concept outcome and invited us to visit him in the Oval Office. Drinking a fine scotch with The Boss in that room was something else. We discussed several interesting things, but I can't tell you about that.

We proved we could do it. We've done it several times since. Now we're fully ready for a combat drop. I'll let you know when that finally happens.

PLEASE POST A REVIEW FOR DAEDALUS SQUAD

ON

AMAZON.COM AND GOODREADS.COM

I really appreciate you posting a review on Amazon and Goodreads. Posting to Amazon.com is intuitive. To post a review on Goodreads.com, click on this link, or go to their website, and become a member if you are not already one. Search for *Daedalus Squad*, and click on the "Want to read" button under the image of *Daedalus Squad*. Indicate that you have read *Daedalus Squad* and then you will be able to post a review. Thank you very much for going through this effort!

EXCERPT FROM THE FIRST CHAPTER OF: SLINGSHOT

by

Robert G. Williscroft

EQUATORIAL PACIFIC—SOUTHEAST OF BAKER ISLAND

Margo stopped kicking her feet as the ominous gray shapes flashed into her peripheral view. Long, tawny hair floated past her head as her feet dropped below her slim, brightly clad body. She took a deep breath and floated slightly upward. A hint of fear crept into her mind as she turned toward three gray, sleek predators cruising just inside the limit of her vision, about twenty-five meters away.

A gentle touch on her shoulder startled her. She turned to see Alex Regent tapping the depth reading on his dive-console with his index finger. Margo reached down and grasped her console, turning it so she could read her depth: twenty-five meters. She had drifted upward five meters since seeing the sharks.

Margo exhaled angrily and let some air out of her breathing bag. She knew better than to lose track of her depth. Out there, her life depended on a constant awareness of exactly how deep she was. Together she and Alex sank back to thirty meters. Off to their right, the three gray shapes drifted with them. Would she ever get used to it, she thought, as she released a bit of air into her bag to stop her descent.

"Alex," she said.

There was no response.

"Alex!" She tapped the back of her console several times.

"Alex!" Nothing but silence.

Alex placed himself in front of Margo and looked into her facemask. With his right hand, he formed a circle with thumb and forefinger. His three other fingers extended straight up.

Margo returned the sign indicating she was all right while nodding vigorously. Then she pointed to her ear and lifted her console, tapping the back. Alex fumbled at his ear and then tapped his console, and then shook his head.

Great, Margo thought, *EFCom is busted just when we really need it. Not busted,* she corrected herself, *just a submerged antenna*. She pointed to the three menacing shapes off to her right. Alex turned and scanned around them. Above and just behind them the blue-painted hull of their boat bobbed in the gentle waves. About twenty meters ahead of them hung a smooth, horizontal fluorescent orange tube about one meter in diameter. To the left, it stretched into the gloom; to the right, it angled downward. The fluorescent tube was attached to a slender cable angling up to the shadow of a buoy just beneath the surface to their right. Alex turned back toward Margo, making an exaggerated shrug.

Margo reached for her dive-console again and pressed a button located prominently on its face. The three sharks turned and commenced a meandering movement toward the two divers. Their front fins extended stiffly downward at about forty-five degrees. Their backs arched slightly, and their blunt snouts moved back and forth as they approached.

Margo felt her hair stand up on the nape of her neck. She turned to Alex and motioned him to her side. Alex withdrew a telescoped baton from its holder at his waist and extended it to its full one-and-a-half-meter length. He checked the safety lever near its handle, and with his thumb he flicked the lever so it pointed forward. As the sharks drew nearer, he held the stick out in front of him, pointed in their direction. Margo glanced around them again and pushed her console button once more. Alex waved the stick about slowly and then steadied up on the nearest of the three menacing monsters.

Suddenly, with blurring speed, the nearest shark attacked. Alex struck out with his stick, the jolt of its impact rocking him backward. A sharp crack was followed by a hissing sound as carbon dioxide rushed into the shark's body. In the same moment, flashes of silvery-black streaked from several directions. One of the remaining sharks was struck broadside by a dolphin's blunt nose. In a flash, it disappeared.

The animal Alex had injected rolled on its side and began a crazed, uncontrolled spiral toward the surface thirty meters above them. On its way up, it was hit several times by charging dolphins. It expired of massive embolisms before reaching fifteen meters. In the melee, the third shark vanished.

Margo reached out for Alex, grabbed a handful of breathing bag, and pulled him close to her. She placed the flat of her full-facemask against his and looked deeply into his eyes, as close to a kiss as she could come under the circumstances. Even down here, they were deep blue. Several bubbles escaped from the positive pressure maintained inside their masks and shimmered their way toward the surface, expanding rapidly as they rose.

Like an old-time scuba diver, Margo thought, watching the rising silvery spheres. Instinctively she checked the volume in her breathing bag and glanced at the gauge on her tiny, ultra-high-pressure air flask. She found she was holding her breath, and as she felt the need to breathe, a gentle pressure developed against her back. She pulled back and turned to confront a two-and-a-half-meter-long dolphin nudging her from behind.

It was one of four that had responded to her sonic signal—George, her favorite. The other three dolphins crowded in around the neoprene and nylon suited divers, jostling each other for attention. Margo rubbed the head dome of each and indicated to Alex that he should do the same. Then the two of them turned their attention back to the tube suspended in front of them.

Alex swam to the angled portion and began to search along the tube's length, descending slowly. Margo dropped her arm from George's neck and kicked in Alex's direction, keeping him in sight, but staying between him and the surface. The four cetaceans arrowed toward the surface and grabbed a gulp of air, then settled back down, playfully cycling between Alex and Margo, gently jostling them. About thirty minutes later, Alex motioned Margo to join him. She released a bubble of air from her bag and dropped down beside him. Her console showed a depth of fifty meters. Alex pointed to a five-centimeter rip in the bottom curve of the tube's fluorescent covering.

Margo reached into a deep pocket located on the left leg of her suit and withdrew a role of patching tape. Alex stretched the edges of the tear, and Margo applied a strip of self-sealing tape along the opening. Then she located a small pneumatic valve on the top of the tube and attached a hose from her spare air tank. On a signal from Alex, she released air into the tube, forcing water out through a one-way valve on the underside. She stopped when bubbles escaped from the lower valve.

As the tube rose slowly, Margo held on, keeping track of their progress on her console. They stopped rising when the gauge read thirty meters. Margo felt the tube—it was taut and solid. She tapped the back of her console, listening for the faint rush of sound in her ears. Nothing. She pointed to the back of her console and then her ear, and shook her head. Alex offered another of his exaggerated underwater shrugs and grinned, although the only part of the grin she could see was his crinkled eyes. She grinned back and pointed toward the suspension buoy and their boat, making an angled upward sign with her free hand. Alex nodded, checked his console, and they both headed back, slowly rising as they swam.

Margo saw Alex check his console from time to time, making certain they kept below the ever-changing ceiling limit it calculated for him. Since she had remained shallower than Alex for most of the dive, she knew she would be safe following his lead. She looked around at the four dolphins. Her earlier fright was gone, and she simply enjoyed George's protective nearness and the playful bumps and nudges from the others.

On the surface finally, Alex dropped his facemask down around his neck, fully inflated his bag and grinned at Margo. "Close call down there!"

Margo shoved her facemask down and patted the glistening snout that appeared in front of her. "Thanks, George. I love you too."

The dolphin mewed a pleased response, lifted his body out of the water and backed away, chattering as he went. The other three animals circled at and below the surface, keeping watch over their human charges.

"What happened to the EFCom?" Margo asked. "I expected it to come back online as soon as the antenna surfaced."

"Broken antenna wire, I imagine," Alex answered.

"Storm damage, I'm sure," said Margo, as they turned and headed toward the waiting vessel.

"Probably," agreed Alex. "But that wasn't a burst seam," he added.

"Yeah, maybe the sinking tube snapped the wire."

Actually, tube flotation chambers flooded on a regular basis. They had patched a full ten percent of them since the project started. But it was a bit unusual to find a rip on the tube bottom, and the Electrostatic Field Communication ("EFCom") transceivers on the buoys almost always survived.

⁕

The EFCom buoy nearest the tear had ceased transmitting, and the buoys on either side of the tear had signaled their departure from datum a day earlier. Alex had opted to employ an electrostatic field communication system, because of its clear underwater signal transmission capability that was independent of acoustic conditions, since it didn't rely on sound transmission through the water. Every buoy, each skimmer and floater, and every diver was outfitted with one of the small EFCom transceivers. Alex had inspected the non-transmitting buoy personally during an overflight from Jarvis Island. There was nothing visible on the two kilometers of surface between the buoys; they were closer together, but not so that it was visible to the eye. Nevertheless, the remaining 1,828-odd buoy-suspended kilometers of tube were stressing from the downward pull of the waterlogged section. The buoy near the tear was several meters underwater.

Suspended inside the flotation tube were two virtually impervious, lightweight, hose-like tubes, each about six centimeters in diameter, called vacuum sheaths. Two shallow channels jutted out from the bottom of each vacuum sheath, filled with electronically-controlled suspending magnets. Magnetically suspended inside each vacuum sheath was a five-centimeter tube of segmented soft iron officially called the rotor, but more popularly known as the ribbon, so named from the earliest conceptions back in the 1980s of the Launch Loop inventor, Keith Lofstrom. Alex was eager to check continuity readings to make certain the vacuum sheaths had not breached. They were not yet evacuated, but seawater entry at this stage would seriously delay the entire project. If the EFCom had not crapped out, the tests would already be underway.

Alex glanced ahead at Margo Jackson, cavorting with her four dolphins as they made their leisurely way back to the waiting boat. His field engineer in charge of underwater construction was a remarkable female. Nearly as tall as his own 183 centimeters, her model's slender figure, encased in electric-blue nylon-covered neoprene, seemed to lack feminine curves. He knew differently, of course, having joined her bikini-clad person from time to time for morning swims since the project began over two years ago.

The project—Alex had lived with it for three years before actual construction began. Longer, actually, if you considered dreams—since before the incredible, worldwide bi-millennial celebration when he still was a young boy.

There was the nearly simultaneous publication in America and England of practically identical ideas in 1985. Paul Birch published an article in *The Journal of the British Interplanetary Society*, while in America Keith Lofstrom published his article in a supplement to *The Journal of the Astronautical Sciences*, he recalled. Nobody could agree on the names: Skyrail, Launch Loop, Beanstalk. There were others, but the idea is what counted, the sky-shaking idea that you don't need rockets to get into space.

Newspapers were full of explanations three-and-a-half years ago when the aging president of a computer software giant made the announcement. He would funnel a significant portion of company profits into the consortium. Space travel would become as commonplace and inexpensive as the personal computers his pioneering work had made possible. He went on to outline the easy-to-understand concept.

Imagine a water hose streaming water in a parabolic arch. Deflect the water and funnel it back to the start through a pump, creating a closed system. Make the stream strong enough and the hose light enough, and the entire structure will support itself—the water holding up the hose structure. Now, replace the water with a thin, closed-loop pipe of segmented soft iron. Make it 5,000 kilometers around and accelerate it to orbital velocity with gigantic linear induction motors from two points on the equator 2,000 kilometers apart. The center section of the structure, including both the outgoing and return legs of the loop, will rise to about eighty kilometers above the Earth. Supply access to the upstream end in space with a Kevlar-hung elevator, and you can launch capsules by magnetically coupling them to the rapidly moving pipe of iron.

Slingshot, they called it. The greatest engineering undertaking in the history of the world, they said.

As the on-scene project manager, Alex was responsible for getting the job done, on schedule, on budget. He was building a gossamer structure over 2,500 kilometers long, a frail spider web, completely invisible when viewed from more than a few kilometers. Alex grinned wryly. All *Slingshot* really consisted of was a fancy evacuated tube, a flexible iron pipe, four linear drivers and their power sources, some guy wires, and a couple of elevators. Put that way it seemed simple enough. But, of course, it wasn't simple at all, and for all his skill and engineering competence, and despite surface appearances, deep down Alex was not entirely sure that he could make it happen.

Margo and Alex climbed up the ladder and onto *Skimmer One's* bobbing fantail. This was one of two skimmers on the project—twelve-meter-long surface-effect boats that looked more like a floating aircraft than a traditional motorboat. They were capable of 200 knots, skimming about one-and-a-half meters over the wave tops. They had a small open fantail, just large enough for a couple of divers to doff their gear. Being on the fantail when the skimmer was on its cushion was more than dangerous, and was strictly prohibited throughout the project.

Alex signaled to the waiting coxswain, and they got underway for Baker, plowing through the water while Alex and Margo remained exposed. He and Margo stood near the stern railing and removed their dripping skins. Alex looked back at the buoys, now presumably in their proper places.

"How many more times?" Alex looked quizzically at Margo.

"Who knows?" She glanced back at the bobbing buoys. "We have repair people available at both ends. We shouldn't be doing this ourselves, you know." She turned and looked directly at Alex. "What do you think—weather or sabotage?"

Alex shrugged and tossed the spent carbon dioxide cartridge from his shark stick in the general direction of the cavorting dolphins. "I wanted to see for myself, and I still don't know. Does it matter? We can't patrol the entire eighteen-hundred-twenty-eight-kilometer length anyway."

"What are we dealing with?" Margo asked. "You don't get out here in a rowboat."

"We're two thousand wet klicks from any kind of civilization," Alex said. "At minimum, that's a large motor-yacht or even an ocean sailer—you know, one of those we maybe can afford when this job is done." He sighed. "We're dealing with lots of money and someone with a major bitch."

He looked into her green eyes.

"Just keep my tubes at depth." His blue eyes flashed, and he turned toward the cockpit to radio his orders to test pipe continuity.

✷

Margo dropped her eyes at his challenge. For the thousandth time, she asked herself if she had bitten off more than she could chew with this assignment. Was it her fault that the flotation chambers kept ripping? Was she missing something important? Was she copping out to imply there might have been sabotage? And yet, Alex seemed to agree that it might be sabotage. When she joined the project two years ago, the newspapers had acclaimed her as the ideal role model for the new twenty-first-century woman. At times that burden lay heavily on her shoulders, as it did now, she reflected.

It was a vast responsibility, and there was no way one person actually could control all of it at once. How Alex handled the weight of the entire project awed her, but she was careful never to let him know.

Margo watched Alex step into the cockpit. He was tall and slender, richly tanned from his constant outdoor work. She felt a softness well up inside her, a gentle warmth spreading out from the pit of her stomach. She bit her lower lip and turned angrily to lean on the after-railing.

None of that, she chided herself. This assignment was too important, and the stakes too high, to let any kind of emotion intrude. As she entered the cabin and sealed the port, the skipper switched modes, and pressurized air quickly filled the hard-sided skirt. In moments the skimmer lifted out of the water, except for the port and starboard skirts that protruded about a meter into the waves. Within seconds, high-pressure water nozzles jetted water from the end of each skirt, and within thirty seconds *Skimmer One* was approaching 200 knots.

As *Skimmer One* headed into the afternoon sun, trailing an arrow-straight wake of white foam, Margo stood looking aft through the sealed port, remembering her instinctive sharing, and their underwater kiss following the fright of nearly becoming shark food. She shook off the sensation and busied herself with putting away their diving equipment. But a hint of a smile remained on her lips as they shot over the surface, finally settling back onto the water as they entered the small protected artificial harbor on the west side of Baker Island, just south of a shallow reef that went dry at low tide.

WORDS OF PRAISE FOR *SLINGSHOT*

Slingshot does for the launch loop what Arthur C. Clarke's *The Fountains of Paradise* or Sheffield's *Web Between the Worlds* did for the space elevator. Again, Williscroft delivers a great mix of hard science fiction and action.

— Alastair Mayer
Author of the *T-Space Series*

Robert Williscroft deftly crafts an energetic story around a phenomenal technological development just over the horizon: the space launch loop. The technical detail woven into this story is an education unto itself. But don't assume that Williscroft chooses raw infodump over story—*Slingshot* is an adventure that pulls you in, gives you characters that are engaging, and invites you to follow them through their challenges. What Williscroft has done in *Slingshot* is no easy task—he has balanced the *hard* aspect of science fiction with the character portrayals that those who despise that very *hard* science fiction beg for. The last decade has seen impressive leaps in the theoretical work toward the launch loop—this book couldn't come too soon! And you won't be able to keep from reading all the way to the end. Williscroft's art continues to be praise-worthy!

— Jason D. Batt, *100 Year Starship*
Author of *The Tales of Dreamside series*

I've been a fan of Robert Williscroft's books for a while now. They're action-packed and filled with all kinds of interesting, real-world information. *Slingshot* fits right in.

Slingshot is about the development of an earth-bound spaceport in which spaceships are taken 80 kilometers above the Earth by elevator and hurled onto their trajectory by a very fast-moving ribbon of soft iron. It is much easier, cheaper, and cleaner to launch spaceships from here due to the rarified atmosphere. This concept may be a reality someday. The book begins with a foreword by Keith Lofstrom, the originator of this concept called the "launch loop."

Learning about the launch loop is the most interesting aspect of this novel. Williscroft's descriptions of the construction techniques, its operations, and the benefits for space travel are absolutely fascinating. The book takes place about thirty years in the future, and I could easily see such a project becoming a reality in that time.

The plot of the novel is driven by the development and construction of the project, which is being threatened by ill-informed environmentalists bent on destroying the project. The launch loop is far greener than the current method of launching vehicles into space, but a sinister power has misled the environmentalists into believing that sabotaging the launch loop is saving the planet. Meanwhile, the sinister power is protecting its own economic interests.

As usual, Williscroft has created a cast of interesting and driven characters. The book is a fascinating read, and you are guaranteed not only to learn a lot, but to dream about the future of space travel.

— Marc Weitz, Past President
The Los Angeles Adventurers' Club

Available in hardcover, paperback,
and all ebooks everywhere.

ABOUT THE AUTHOR

Dr. Robert G. Williscroft served twenty-three years in the U.S. Navy and the National Oceanic and Atmospheric Administration (NOAA). He commenced his service as an enlisted nuclear Submarine Sonar Technician in 1961, was selected for the Navy Enlisted Scientific Education Program in 1966, and graduated from University of Washington in Marine Physics and Meteorology in 1969. He returned to nuclear submarines as the Navy's first Poseidon Weapons Officer. Subsequently, he served as Navigator and Diving Officer on both catamaran mother vessels for the Deep Submergence Rescue Vehicle. Then he joined the Submarine Development Group One out of San Diego as the Officer-in-Charge of the Test Operations Group, conducting "deep-ocean surveillance and data acquisition"—which forms the basis for his Cold War novel *Operation Ivy Bells.*

In NOAA Dr. Williscroft directed diving operations throughout the Pacific and Atlantic. As a certified diving instructor for both the National Association of Underwater Instructors (NAUI) and the Multinational Diving Educators Association (MDEA), he taught over 3,000 individuals both basic and advanced SCUBA diving. He authored four diving books, developed the first NAUI drysuit course, developed advanced curricula for mixed gas and other specialized diving modes, and developed and taught a NAUI course on the Math and Physics of Advanced Diving. His doctoral dissertation for California Coast University, *A System for Protecting SCUBA Divers from the Hazards of Contaminated Water* was published by the U.S.

Department of Commerce and distributed to Port Captains worldwide. He also served three shipboard years in the high Arctic conducting scientific baseline studies, and thirteen months at the geographic South Pole in charge of National Science Foundation atmospheric projects.

Dr. Williscroft has written extensively on terrorism and related subjects. He is the author of a popular book on current events published by Pelican Publishing: *The Chicken Little Agenda—Debunking Experts' Lies*, now in its second edition as an eBook, and a new children's book series, *Starman Jones*, in collaboration with Dr. Frank Drake, world-famous director of the Carl Sagan Center for the Study of Life in the Universe and the SETI Institute.

Dr. Williscroft's 1st novel in *The Starchild Trilogy, Slingshot*, tells the story of the construction of the world's first Space Launch Loop. *Slingshot* was launched at the Seattle International Space Elevator Conference in August 2015. His 2nd novel in *The Starchild Trilogy, The Starchild Compact,* is based on the discovery that Saturn's moon Iapetus is actually a derelict starship, and how Earth explorers eventually meet with the "Founders," who originally arrived on the starship and populated the Earth long ago. The 3rd book in *The Starchild Trilogy, The Iapetus Federation*, the Federation expands Solar Systemwide, while a new Caliphate sweeps Earth. The Starchild Institute creates wormhole portals to enable the Exodus. Earth becomes medieval, while human focus shifts to the Iapetus Federation. Humans settle every potentially habitable spot in the Solar System and begin expanding into the rest of the Galaxy.

The Daedalus Files takes place in the world of *Slingshot*. In four short stories, *Daedalus, Daedalus LEO, Daedalus Squad*, and *Daedalus Combat*, Dr. Williscroft follows the U.S. Navy SEALS Winged Insertion Command (SWIC) and its development of the *Gryphon* hard wingsuit for combat drops from Low Earth Orbit

Dr. Williscroft is an active member of the venerable Adventurers' Club of Los Angeles, where he is the former Editor of the Club's monthly magazine. He is a board member of the Colorado Authors' League. He lives in Centennial, Colorado, with his wife, Jill, whom he met upon his return from the South Pole in 1982 and finally married in 2011, and their twin college boys (when they are home from school).

OTHER WORKS BY
ROBERT G. WILLISCROFT

Please visit Amazon.com to discover other eBooks by Robert Williscroft and your favorite online or Brick & Mortar bookseller for their paper versions:

Current events:

The Chicken Little Agenda—Debunking "Experts"' Lies

Children's books:

The Starman Jones Series:

Starman Jones: A Relativity Birthday Present
Starman Jones Goes to the Dogs (scheduled for release in 2019)

Short Stories:

The Daedalus Files:

Daedalus
Daedalus—LEO
Daedalus—Squad
Daedalus—Combat (scheduled for release in 2019)

Novels:

Mac McDowell Missions:

Operation Ivy Bells
Operation Snow Cone (Scheduled for release 2020)

The Starchild Trilogy:

Slingshot

The Starchild Compact

The Iapetus Federation

The Oort Chronicles:

Icicle—A Tensor Matrix (scheduled for release in 2019)

The Oort—Interstellar Consequences (scheduled for release in 2020)

Oort Andromeda—Galactic Diaspora (scheduled for release in 2020)

CONNECT WITH ROBERT G. WILLISCROFT

I really appreciate you reading my book! Here are my social media coordinates:

Friend me on Facebook: *https://www.facebook.com/robert.williscroft*
Follow me on Twitter: *@RGWilliscroft*
Like my Amazon author page: *http://www.amazon.com/Robert-G.-Williscroft/e/B001JP52AS*
Subscribe to my blog: *Thrawn Rickle http://ThrawnRickle.com*
Connect on LinkedIn: *http://www.linkedin.com/in/argee/*
Visit my website: *http://robertwilliscroft.com*

DAEDALUS SQUAD GLOSSARY

Baker Compound—The *Slingshot* facility on Baker Island.

BatCap—Power source for the Pulsed Energy Weapon, a unique marriage of a 3-D battery and a thin, large-surface-area flexible capacitor that the SWIC member wears on his back. The capacitor supports twenty rapid-release lethal laser bursts and recharges in less than a minute from the 3-D battery, or it can continuously support a lethal laser burst every five seconds. The 3-D battery needs recharging every five thousand bursts.

EMT—Emergency Medical Technician.

Gryphon-7—A wingsuit-like carapace strapped on the body. It stopped short of the feet, but in flight could extend to a full two meters, stretching beyond the feet. It attached to the legs and arms, with special controls for each hand, and had a broad Velcro band across the midriff. It had extensible delta wings with a three-meter wingspan. The back end contained a small steerable hypergolic rocket engine, and the left and right wings each contained pressurized hypergolic fuel components. Switches in the hand units controlled the fuel valves. The *Gryphon* had a heads-up display with height-over-ground, airspeed, groundspeed, compass, and GPS coordinates superimposed on a map, plus various system readouts.

Gryphon-10—Like *Gryphon-7* with some radical changes including full body armor with circulating fuel for heat protection, an increased surface area using dimples, wrinkles, and rolls that dramatically boosted heat shedding, and it incorporated a new type of polymer that was stronger, lighter, and more heat resistant than anything before. The biggest change was Mother, the guidance computer unit designed to act on its calculations before the human pilot was even aware of them. Still man-transportable, although more ungainly than *Gryphon-7*. Its unpowered glide ratio was 14-1, and it could fly 100 level klicks under power.

Gryphon-10, Mk 4—Looked exactly like the *Gryphon-10*. It differed in subtle ways because of improvements developed during several LEO drops. Incorporated the latest model of a very efficient, hand-held, pulsed energy weapon into a node in the leading edge of either the left or right wing. Its power source is a lightweight BatCap. Before opening the carapace after landing, the SWIC member retrieves the weapon from its node and holsters it just like a sidearm.

Howland Island—A coral island in the equatorial Pacific about sixty-five kilometers north of Baker Island. It was the destination of Amelia Earhart when she disappeared.

HP oxygen—High-pressure oxygen

Hypergolic fuel– Fuel that ignites spontaneously when the individual fuel elements come into contact.

Hypergolic rocket or jet– A rocket or jet that uses hypergolic fuel.

Keith Lofstrom—Inventor of the Launch Loop.

Kick thruster—A small, reigniteable solid-state rocket attached to a capsule, used for vector changes after release from the rail, or to slow down a capsule used to transit from Baker to Jarvis. The rocket was extinguished with an iris-like very strong magnetic field that sliced through the solid fuel column just above the burn.

Klick—Slang word for kilometer.

Launch Loop—A means for getting into space without using rockets.

Launch Loop International—The company that and manages Slingshot.

Launch pouch—Attaches to the capsule underside, enabling magnetic acceleration of the capsule up the Skytower or by the rail.

Mach number—The ratio of the speed of a body to the speed of sound in the surrounding medium.

Nitrogen tetroxide—A hypergolic fuel component (see UDMH).

Pallet—A regular cargo pallet used to transport cargo up the Skytower and along the rail for launch into orbit. Each pallet carried four tanks. Two were HP oxygen used by the flyer until Gryphon separation, attached to the wingsuit with breakaway connectors. The other two carried hypergolic fuel, UDMH and nitrogen tetroxide, for the small hypergolic maneuvering jets

Pulsed Energy Weapon—Fires pulsed high-energy laser bursts. Is virtually silent.

Rail—Common term for the portion of the launch loop between the skyports.

Ribbon—Common term for the soft-iron tube that is the heart of the launch loop.

SEAL—An acronym for *Sea Air and Land*; a member of a Naval Special Warfare unit trained for unconventional warfare.

Skyport—The structure at the top of the skytower.

Skyrail—An alternative name for a Space Elevator or Launch Loop.

Skytower—The elevator-like set of cables that extends from the Skyport to the socket below.

Slingshot—The Space Launch Loop between Baker and Jarvis Islands in the equatorial Pacific.

Socket—The attachment point at the bottom of the skytower.

SWIC—SEALS Winged Insertion Command

UDMH—Unsymmetrical dimethylhydrazine, a hypergolic fuel component (see nitrogen tetroxide).

UV light—Ultraviolet light.

Wingsuit -Aa suit with fabric filling the gaps between stretched out arms and ankles, and between the legs, enabling the wearer to glide through the air.

Fresh Ink Group

Independent Multi-media Publisher

Fresh Ink Group / Push Pull Press

ꝏ

Hardcovers
Softcovers
All Ebook Platforms
Audiobooks
Worldwide Distribution

ꝏ

Indie Author Services
Book Development, Editing, Proofing
Graphic/Cover Design
Video/Trailer Production
Website Creation
Social Media Management
Writing Contests
Writers' Blogs
Podcasts

ꝏ

Authors
Editors
Artists
Experts
Professionals

ꝏ

FreshInkGroup.com
info@FreshInkGroup.com
Twitter: @FreshInkGroup
Facebook.com/FreshInkGroup
LinkedIn: Fresh Ink Group

www.ingramcontent.com/pod-product-compliance
Lightning Source LLC
Chambersburg PA
CBHW070454170726
48291CB00005B/1742

* 9 7 8 1 9 4 7 8 6 7 6 2 8 *